The Sax

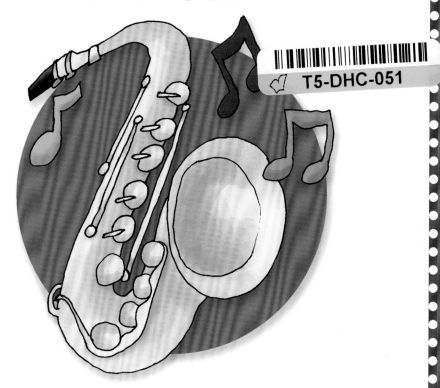

by Susan Hartley • illustrated by Anita DuFalla

Ben saw the sax.

"No! My sax!" he said.

Ben was sad.

Ben went to see Max and Rex.
"Can you fix my sax?"
said Ben.

3

"We will see if we can fix the sax," said Max.

"Do not be sad," said Rex.

"You can mix this for Tex."

"This is fun to do," said Ben.
"I like to mix this for Tex.
But I am sad for my sax."

Ben went home.

He was sad.

Ben saw Bob. Bob said,
"Ben, here is a box for you."

Ben saw the sax.
"This is good! I am
not sad now!" said Ben.